I COULD SEE NOTHING
SETTLING WEST TEXAS

I COULD SEE NOTHING

Settling West Texas

*By Mary Lou Crump Koehler
and Lou Anna Koehler*

Copright © 2017 by Mary Lou Koehler

All Rights Reserved

Published by Lou Anna Koehler
west.tx.history@gmail.com

The scanning, uploading, and distribution of this book via
the internet or any other means without express permission
of the publisher is illegal and punishable by law. Please do
not participate in or support the electronic piracy of copy-
righted materials.
Your support is appreciated.

First Printing Hard Back May 2018
ISBN 13: 978-0998970431
ISBN 10: 0998970433

First Printing Paper Back August 2017
ISBN 13: 978-0998970400
ISBN 10: 0998970409

PUBLISHED IN THE USA

DEDICATION

In the nineteen thirties my folks took my sister and myself with them to the Settlers' picnics in Lubbock County. The Pioneer Settlers enjoyed greeting friends and swapping stories about the past.

I dedicate this book to the Settlers.

PAPA AND MARY LOU

I COULD SEE NOTHING CONTENTS

CHAPTER 1 TEEPEES AT DRY FORK CREEK 1

CHAPTER 2 PROSPECTING FOR A NEW HOME. 7

CHAPTER 3 A TRAIN RIDE TO BIG D AND BEYOND 17

CHAPTER 4 CHRISTMAS STORIES 29

CHAPTER 5 A LONG COLD DAY 33

CHAPTER 6 WASH DAY. 37

CHAPTER 7 PRAIRIE FIRE 39

CHAPTER 8 FUN AND GAMES. 43

EPILOGUE. 49

I Could See Nothing

Chapter 1 Teepees at Dry Fork Creek

Howdy, folks. This story starts back in 1886, in Henrietta, Texas. My name is Bob and I was six years old back then. My parents, eight year old brother Dave, four year old sister Mamie, and I were happy in our town. It was the county seat of Clay County and 100 miles from Dallas, where our grandparents lived. We sometimes took the train there for a family visit. This story tells of our family's move to the town of Benjamin, Texas, and then a move to Lubbock County on the High Plains in 1890, where we grew up to be adults.

Henrietta had a two-story brick schoolhouse with a large playground, four churches, two drug stores, a jail, a bank, two livery stables, a blacksmith shop, opera house, and a large courthouse. Papa had a store that sold general merchandise, but mostly groceries. He bought all the food in bulk. He sold crackers from a barrel. Molasses, vinegar, and pickles came in large crock containers. Dried fruits, salt, soda, and flour came in sturdy wooden boxes or cloth sacks. Lick, as lard was called then, was sold from a large tin can. Dried strips of beef jerky were popular. He stocked soap, matches, and coal oil for lamps and stoves. A dozen or maybe more cigars came packed in a little wooden box. Dave and I had our pictures on the lid of each cigar box. Mama had sent our pictures to the cigar company and they printed them on the boxes that Papa was going to sell.

You could smell the pickles when you walked into the store and up on a high shelf he had two big jars full of candy. Ranch women came in their buggies to shop and cowboys would stop in to buy dried fruit and jerky to put in their saddlebags.

The most popular place on the main street was the train station. The friendly agent there enjoyed teasing the children who came to watch the trains. He wore a cap with a bill and a vest with a watch in the pocket. The watch had a long chain that was attached to a buttonhole on his vest. I think the watch was gold.

THE CIGAR BOX COVER

We children played on the dusty main street and at the school playground, drawing cattle brands in the dirt, bouncing balls, shooting marbles, or coasting down the hill to the railroad station in a little wooden wagon. The favorite marble games were Seven Up and Rolly Holy. To play Seven Up, you place four marbles to make a square, with each marble about 10 inches apart and one marble in the center of the square. Two players, each with their own marbles, shoot at the five marbles and when a player hits a marble he gets to take it out of game. The one with the most marbles wins. Rolly Holy was a fun game. A little hole is made in the center of a three-foot dirt circle and the players shoot for the hole. The goal is to get the most marbles in the hole in the center of the circle. Curl the finger that's next to your thumb to hold the marble and use your thumb to shoot it. Dave could really make a marble fly. Main Street and the school playground were fun places to play.

We lived in a four-room house that faced west and had a

I COULD SEE NOTHING

swing on the porch. We sure enjoyed pushing each other in the porch swing. We would get the swing going high and jump out to the front of the yard. The game was to see who could sail the furthest and it was always Dave. Papa dug a cellar under the kitchen with the entrance on the outside of the house. The space was used to store vegetables for the winter and firewood. There was a cistern for water with a rope over a pulley to let the bucket up and down. Dave and I took turns pulling up water for the family. That bucket was heavy when it was full. Mother kept a water bucket and dipper on the front porch for us to drink from. We didn't have any glass in the windows, only a shutter to open and close. In the summer the shutter was always open. The toilet was an outhouse several feet from the back door. It had a built in bench with a large hole. Our bathtub was a square galvanized tub that we put in the center of the kitchen floor every Saturday night. It was filled half full with cold water first, then Mama would heat a kettle of water on the stove and pour it in to heat the water up a bit. We drew straws to see who got to bathe first. That last one had to wash in some pretty dirty water after a long week of playing.

The most excitement for me was when the Indians came to town. You could see the dust from their wagons miles away. They came from Fort Sill. Back then it was Indian Territory and eventually it became Oklahoma. Their wagons were loaded with bones. The bones were from cows, horses, buffalo, and other animals that died on the prairie from lack of food, disease, old age, or cold. Indians were paid eight to ten dollars a ton for bones. The bones were shipped by rail to the South where they were ground into fertilizer for the farmers. The Indians bought supplies to haul back to the reservation.

The Indians made camp along the creek near town. Dave and I watched from a high limb on a big pecan tree one time when they came. They unharnessed the horses for a drink in the creek and began to make camp. They cut poles from the cottonwood trees and stretched canvas over them to make tee-pees. The women built campfires with sticks they picked up. A few soldiers from the Fort came with the Indians. The Indians

TEEPEES

wore mostly leather clothing.

The rattle of the Indians' wooden wagons moving to the railroad station awakened me early next morning. We hurried through breakfast and soon Dave, Papa, and I were on our way to watch the unloading of the wagons. The Indians were tossing the bones into open boxcars. Some of their kids had come along and were hanging around the tracks trying to balance on the slick rails.

I noticed a girl about my age with black braids that hung all the way to her waist and her arms were covered with beautiful silver bracelets. I was sure she was a princess. There was only one way to find out, so I balanced myself on the rails and walked over.

"Where did you get all those bracelets"? I asked. She turned away. I only wanted a closer look. The Fort Worth and Denver agent saw me looking at those bracelets and he grabbed my arm and pulled me toward an Indian wagon.

"I'll trade this boy for that pretty Indian girl," he said in a loud voice. I struggled hard to get away but he caught me by the seat of the pants and lifted me off the ground. "He's not very big but you can see from his kicks that he's strong, don't you want to trade?" Fear jumped in my heart and I finally wiggled free. I ran in a panic for Papa's wagon and I could hear people laughing behind me. I should have known that the

I COULD SEE NOTHING

Indians wouldn't trade, why those bracelets alone were worth more than a six-year-old white boy.

I remember another time when the Indians were in town. We were eating dinner and Papa was not at home. All of a sudden an Indian stuck his head through the open window. He had long black braids and was missing a few teeth. What a scare! I could feel my scalp going all tight. He was selling pecans he had picked up under the trees at Dry Fork Creek. Mama bought a few pecans from him.

The Indians held a war dance one afternoon on the Court House lawn. All the town folks turned out to watch. They sang their whoops and danced up and down in time with the drums. We kids jumped and swung to the beat. During one of the noisy dances, a prisoner broke out of the nearby jail. The jailor fired two shots in the air and the crowd ran in panic, scattering in all directions. I kept just in sight of Papa's coat-tail, running for dear life. Exhausted and scared, I finally got close enough to grab hold of the back of his coat and a face glanced down at me – it was not Papa!

ॐ

Mary Lou Crump Koehler

Mama

I COULD SEE NOTHING

CHAPTER 2 PROSPECTING FOR A NEW HOME

Papa had the roaming spirit of the early pioneer. He was always prospecting, as he called it, but his prospecting was not for gold or silver, but for productive land to own. He questioned every trader or traveler who stopped by his little grocery store: "Which way have you been?" "How high is the grass?" "Where does that country get its water supply?" "Is there a railroad near the area?" "Is it a good spot for a town?" The Plains of Texas was just opening up to settlers at the time.

We finally moved to Benjamin, a nice little town. Our family was growing; my baby sister Kit was born just after we moved. I liked Benjamin. There were pecan trees to climb, swings at the schoolhouse, and a creek to catch our rocks. I could throw almost as far as Dave, now. He was twelve and I was ten. Mama was busy with our two little sisters but Papa let us boys help out in the store. Papa even put pictures of Dave and me on the boxes of cigars again, although people didn't always recognize us because we were so dressed up in the picture. Most days Dave and I wore bib overalls and high top shoes. I just did not see why Papa wanted to keep on "prospecting" for a new homestead, I liked living in Benjamin.

We woke early one spring morning and Mama had packed a big lunch. Papa had said the night before to pack lots of food for this newest prospecting trip. He wanted to get an early start and was anxious to take a look at the "high plains country". Papa had heard the grass was over a foot high on flat land with no breaks; now that was a country he wanted to see.

"Take care of the womenfolk, boys," Papa said. Dave and I both must have grown two inches as he tousled our hair. Mama was smiling, but for some reason her ninety-pound body looked frail today and I was glad she had Dave and me.

7

Goodbyes were thrilling as we were already looking forward to Papa's return, and for Papa, the prospect of finding a better life for his family made the journey even more exciting. I waved until the last bit of the dust kicked up by the team was gone from the road and then took off to the creek.

PAPA AND OLD DAN

On the third day out, after the team had made a strenuous pull up a long steep two-rut road, Papa and the team reached the Caprock, a good 3000 feet above sea level. He said out loud to himself and the team, "This is the country I have been looking for, ever since I came to Texas." Papa had left his home in Kentucky after the Civil War and ended up in Dallas, Texas, where he met Mama. His excited voice rang with a tone of fulfillment as he admired the beautiful expanse of grassland ready for ranching. "Look how flat! A person can see for miles. You wouldn't have to ranch if you didn't want to; this land is perfect for farming." A new challenge grew in his heart and plans to claim a piece of this land developed as he drove the team home. When he finally arrived, he told us our future home would be in Lubbock County, on the Plains.

It was a busy time for our family! Papa sold his store and house items were packed and stored. Mama and the two girls

I COULD SEE NOTHING

went by train to Dallas to stay with the grandparents until Papa and us boys found a new home in Lubbock County.

It was late April 1890 when we began to load the wagon for our trip to a new country. The food was the important thing as far as Dave and I were concerned, and we were glad to load it. It took many trips from the house to fill the 'grub box'. There was a slab of bacon, a box of soda, a tin can of baking powder, a sack of salt, dried beans, dried peaches and apples, raisins, pecans, a jug of molasses, crackers, and potatoes. Papa toted the fifty-pound sack of flour out to the wagon. I was sure we had plenty of food, but I was worried about Papa's cooking ability. Gosh knows Dave and I couldn't cook. I carefully packed the Dutch oven and lid, cast iron skillet, tin plates, cups, and flatware while Papa rolled up the bedding and folded our clothes into a box. We were in a hurry to get started, "Let's go, Papa; hitch up the horses," we shouted. But it was a good thing Papa took time to check, for in our hurry we had forgotten to tie the ten-gallon wooden keg of water onto the wagon. Dan and Rod were our family's team of horses. While they worked hard for Papa, Dave and I considered them to be our pets. "Get-e up," Papa called, and with a slap of the reins we were off — traveling the old two-rut road. Papa drove the team slowly at first giving old Dan and Rod time to warm up. He soon whacked them with the reins again and they speeded up, leaving a cloud of dust hanging behind us. We bounced and jolted as we rode along. The sun warmed our skin and the wind tossed our hair.

"The elephant said to the kangaroo, one more river to cross." We sang as we began to live this exciting adventure. "Froggy went a courting," was another song we sang off key, and we made up verses as we rode along in the creaking, groaning wagon. There wasn't much else to do as we traveled except to wave at the few horseback riders and drivers of the wagons we met. Dave and I kept up the arm waving until they were out of sight. We passed a few homes several miles out of Benjamin and after that, the ride became long and lonesome. The wagon scared up a few jackrabbits and we kept an eye out for snakes.

9

Every once in awhile we would cross a little creek, and those creeks were a welcome stop to rest the horses and to eat. We tied the horses to a live oak tree. I would pat old Dan, pull a big handful of long grass for him, and whisper secrets into his ear while Dave tended Rod. We picked up sticks for the campfire and it was quick to start. Papa would fry bacon and potatoes and bake biscuits in the covered Dutch oven while the fire crackled. Just the smell of the food took away all doubts we might have had about Papa's cooking. The dried fruit was a good ending to a meal, it left a sweet taste in our mouths. We spread our bedrolls on the ground and put our shoes on the wagon in hopes that nothing would crawl into them during the night. The spring air was cool. I wrapped the quilt tightly around my body and watched the bright stars until I fell asleep. The horses began stomping around at sunrise and this woke Dave and I. The sun was coming up bright and beautiful. The horses grazed around our camp while Papa cooked us flapjacks. After, we got an early start to the day.

WINDMILLS ALONG THE WAY

On our second day out we spotted a windmill and when we finally reached it, Papa refilled the wooden water keg. The windmill brings water up from the ground and into a pipe. The water from the pipe fills a tank with water for cattle. Dave and I drank from the pipe. A cowboy with a big smile rode up, and we learned from him that we were on the 8 Ranch, known

I COULD SEE NOTHING

in later years as the "6666". The cowboy turned up the brim of his big hat, filled it with water and drank. Dave and I chuckled; we never thought a hat would make a water cup. The ranches were big, back then, with no fences. Cattle were branded so the cowboys could easily tell which cows belonged to which ranch. There were all kinds of brands; XIT, IOA, HM, and OJ. I bet Dave that I could spot the next windmill first, and I did. It was at the Pitch Fork Ranch headquarters.

We stopped for a rest there, and Dave and I were happy to see two boys about our own age. We watered Dan and Rod at the horse trough. The boys were interested in our ride from Benjamin. They knew about the bleached buffalo skeletons that we had counted, snakes, coyotes, buzzards, and jackrabbits. The saddle ponies in the corral took my eye and I thought how lucky it would be to live on a ranch. All too soon Papa was hitching up the team to leave. Dave and I hated to wave goodbye to our new friends.

We talked like such brave men to the boys at the ranch. Only Dan, the horse, knew how I really felt at night as I lay under the stars listening to the lonesome howl of the coyote, or on the day we saw a big buzzard eating a dead calf, or when a hawk flew by, clutching a small bleeding rabbit. This was a new experience and at times I felt afraid. I don't think Dave worried about our future.

We spotted the third windmill on the third day, on the Hank Smith place in Blanco Canyon. We could see a house in the distance. The house was made of rocks. We had not seen many rock houses and this was a big one. We wondered where all those rocks had come from; it would take lots of wagons to bring in enough rocks to build this house. This old rock house had been a stopping place for traders and buffalo hunters ever since it was built in 1776, we learned. How I wished that the old house could talk! I would have liked to hear all the stories it knew about Indians and buffalo hunts!

It was on the first day of May 1890, that we made our final climb to the top of the Caprock. When we reached the top all I could see was ... NOTHING! There were no hills or trees and no windmills. Dave and I could not see the beauty Papa had prepared us to see. He had told us that this was the country he had been looking for ever since he came to Texas. There was nothing to break the view as far as your eye could see. A herd of antelope was surprised to see us and with speed and grace they glided off through the knee-high grass, their white tails waving goodbye.

A Plains Rock House

Our first night in this flat country we tried to look busy, but Papa pretty soon reminded us to gather the "prairie coal". We were surprised to learn that prairie coal was nothing but old dry dung. Dave and I had to hustle about, picking up buffalo and cow chips to build our campfire. We filled a gunnysack, and that was enough for Papa to cook supper. This was a strange way to cook, I thought. Over dung? I hoped it wouldn't flavor the food.

We had to hobble the horses so they could not wander away during the night, since there was nothing to tether them to. Their front legs were tied together with a short length of rope. They could move around to graze, but they couldn't run off.

The next morning we woke to the sound of bob white, bob-white, bob-bob-white. We soon saw a flock of bobwhite quail at the edge of the camp. That afternoon a lake came into sight, much to my surprise. Dave and I talked about fishing. We did

I Could See Nothing

not have a fishing pole but maybe we could catch a fish with our hands. We could cook it for supper, we were tired of bacon. Papa listened quietly as we daydreamed of fishing. Papa must be blind if he could not see the lake, I thought. Then a cowboy came into view, riding through the lake. It must not be very deep. Odd. The horse was not swimming and he was not splashing up water as he loped along. We soon caught up with the rider and we were puzzled to find the ground, man, and horse dry. Papa told us we had seen a mirage. He explained that a mirage is an optical illusion caused by the reflection of light through layers of air of different temperatures. You never reach a mirage and people say that some lost travelers have died of thirst from following a mirage. Guess no fish for supper.

Fellow Traveler

The cowboy wished us well and we parted with a wave. It was good to know that we would see people on the Plains. We stopped by a dirt tank that was filled by a windmill. A big crane flew away and near the edge of the water, a big bull snake that had come for a drink was sunning on the bank.

We stopped at Estacado, a town with a population of one or two hundred people. The town was well established with a Quaker church, a general store, a doctor, and an academy.

Papa rented a room in which to store our things and began to make plans for a trip to Amarillo. We would need to store our belongings until we found a more permanent home. Amarillo, Texas was located on the Fort Worth and Denver railroad line and we would be able to buy supplies we'd need to set up a new home. Papa, being a shopkeeper himself, made arrangements with the local store to pick up supplies the owner needed for his store. This would give us a full wagonload and would help out with our traveling expenses.

We climbed into the old wagon again for the 125-mile trip to Amarillo. We were told the freight trip took three days going and about four or six coming back with a full load. I had heard a lot of tales about this Panhandle town. Some said that it was the only place in the world where a cowboy could stand in snow up to his neck and still get sand in his eyes. Still others said that they would someday discover the North Pole in Amarillo, Texas.

The jackrabbits looked big and fast and were fun to watch as we rode along the lonely road again. We watered the horses in small surface lakes that had been filled by the early spring rain. Dave was the first to sight the town of Plainview late on the first evening. We were seeing towns for a change! There was another town with a great deal of barking and chattering but we had to look quickly to catch sight of the "townspeople". It was a prairie dog town and the little squirrel-like animals chattered away at each other as they ran in and out of their holes. We saw one big prairie dog facing a group of five or six and barking out a message, which Dave insisted must have been a sermon. The prairie dogs were fun to watch. We pointed out their holes to Papa and he steered the horses around them.

The coyotes still howled every night as we camped out on the prairie. Dave and I would catch little horned toads and play with them on the wagon, then turn them loose when we rode by an anthill. They ate ants. Papa still cooked over the cow and buffalo chips that Dave and I picked up, but most of the excitement I had felt a week ago was gone. I missed Mama but only Dan knew it. It's nice to have a horse that

I Could See Nothing

understands a fellow. The sunsets and sunrises over the open flat plain of the prairie were the most brilliant I'd ever seen – I guess because there was nothing to block the view. The bright colors lighted the sky; they were always changing and added beauty to the prairie.

NIGHTTIME SERENADE

We were glad to finally reach the regular freight wagon stop, Happy Holler. Wagons full of freight were stopped at Happy Holler when we rolled in. One six horse team was pulling a string of three wagons. The driver was glad to tell us how the Holler got its name. During the rainy season an awful mud hole softens up. Drivers were "happy" when they could cross this "hollow" without getting stuck. A wagon stuck in mud would be a big mess for the horses and the men who would have to pull and shove it onto firmer ground. I was happy that we had a Happy wagon stop. There were food, water, and wagon parts for sale at this freight stop in Happy. The freight wagons hauled supplies from Amarillo to the little towns and ranches in the area.

As we neared Amarillo, Palo Duro Canyon looked pretty with its green cedar trees and the river running through it. Papa told us the river was a branch of the Red River. This canyon furnished a pleasant change of scenery after our days on the plains. We saw more deer, birds, including wild turkeys, and there were even fish in the river. We all took a quick bath in the cold water. Dave grabbed the towel first for a rub down and left it wet and cold for me. Papa got clean clothes for us out of the wagon and we were soon on our way again. Rolling into Amarillo, Papa saw a man he knew and gave him a wave. The man had only one arm and seemed glad to see Papa. He invited us to come with him to Deaf Smith County; he planned to start a town. Papa shook his head no. "Come with me to Lubbock County," he told the man with a grin. "We are going to start a town". This was first time I had heard Papa mention that he planned to help start a town. A town in this nothing, nothing land made me shake my head. I wondered how that man from Deaf Smith County had lost his arm.

WILD TURKEYS

When we returned from Amarillo we camped at the Singer store in Yellow House Canyon. That was several miles from what is now the town of Lubbock. There was also a post office for traders, hunters, other prospectors, and ranchmen. This was the start of the town of Lubbock. That's an interesting story all its own. The "nothing nothing" land turned out to be a fine place to live. Papa moved a little one-room house from Estacado on two wagons and he then went on to build on a second room.

Chapter 3 A Train Ride to Big D and Beyond

I'm Mamie. Mama, me, and baby Kit took the train to Dallas to stay with Grandpa and Grandma King and Mother's sister Aunt Matt, while Papa and the boys made their way to West Texas to find our new home.

"Come on, Mama, get on the train," I said and tugged at her skirt the day we left. The train had rattled to a full stop and steam came rolling out of the engine. I wanted to sit by the window. Papa laid baby Kit on the seat facing me, gave Mama a kiss goodbye and a big hug for me. "I will be a good girl, Papa," I told him. I waved to Dave and Bob from the window as the train jumped forward with a jerk and chug chug we were on our way.

THE TRAIN

This was not my first train ride to Dallas. We'd gone to visit Grandpa and Grandma King before. It was a wonderful way to travel. A nice man sold apples, candy, and dried fruit. We could sleep in our seats. My seat was by the window and Mama had Kit wrapped tight in a blanket. Mama fussed with the baby's blanket and made her a comfortable bed on the seat. We would stay with Grandpa and Grandma King and Aunt Matt until Papa had us our house in the new country. I loved my visits in Dallas. Last visit Grandpa got me a primer and taught me to read. I wasn't even five yet. I hoped we would read again this visit. Maybe Grandpa would buy me another book, a big thick one, now that I was eight.

I remember a fair in Dallas. Grandpa and I took the streetcar. There was a big cowboy statue; I had to look way up to see the top. There was a trough at the bottom of the statue filled with little boats and tiny ships sailing around in the water. I loved seeing the little boats; the blue one was my favorite. We visited the barn to see the cows and horses. There were pretty dresses and quilts on display and some of them won red, blue, or white ribbons. There were people, people everywhere; walking, talking, and laughing. It was fun to come to this big Dallas fair. We rode the streetcar home, after. Grandpa told me to look at the red clay as we rode by. I knew a boy named Clay. My brothers told me his folks named him that because he wallowed in red clay dirt but I don't think that was true. I thought of all my happy memories of Dallas and couldn't wait to get there as we rode on in the train.

Grandpa's brother, Uncle Jeff, lived in Dallas too. I hoped we would see him. On my last visit he came over one night and brought me candy in a sack. I was so anxious to look inside the sack that I got too close to the candle and singed my hair. We all three had a nap on the train and then it was time to eat the lunch Mama had packed for us. Mama gave me a nickel to buy a chocolate bar from a man selling apples, oranges, and candy. He carried his wares all through the train on a big tray. I picked out a special candy bar wrapped in blue paper, yum yum!

AUNT MATT

Grandpa met us at the train station and we took the streetcar home. The house was big. It had an upstairs, a big front porch, and a beautiful parlor downstairs. Aunt Matt had her piano in the parlor. We three had a bedroom upstairs with pretty pink curtains. Grandma had put a fresh flower in a vase on the washstand and that made me feel special. The yard was filled with trees and good smelling flowers.

The milkman came early. I liked his horse. The horse was named Dan just like our horse back at home. He left two big bottles of milk and we gave him back two empty bottles. Next came the ice man. He carried a big block of ice with a pair of large tongs and placed it in the icebox in the kitchen. He had a big black horse but he did not tell me the horse's name. I put milk on my oatmeal every morning. Oatmeal was not my favorite breakfast. Grandma insisted I eat all the oatmeal and that would make me a suffering hero and one day people would write about me in books.

Baby Kit

I sat with Grandpa on the porch while he read his paper. Kit enjoyed being on the porch, too. Grandma would rock her and she liked watching the streetcar go by. We would say "streetcar streetcar," to Kit when it did. One morning she plainly said "streetcar" to our surprise and then she didn't say another word for a long time. That was a big word to be Kit's first word.

MAMIE

I could have big person talks with Grandpa. We talked about miracles. I thought a miracle would be Papa finding us a pretty house on the prairie. Grandpa disagreed, he told me a miracle would be a "cow sitting on a cactus singing like a mockingbird".

I watched for the mailman every day. Mama was excited when we had a letter from Papa. Papa, Dave, and Bob were moving all our things in our wagon from Benjamin to find

I COULD SEE NOTHING

our new place. Papa said the Plains are flat and this was the country he had been looking for. I think he planned to start a town. Mama said she hoped the boys would stay dry and not get sick. I guess if it rained, they could sleep under the wagon. She told Bob to "watch it" and not fall off the wagon. Dave said they would see rattlesnakes, maybe a hundred. Papa was going to find a house for us. Then we would take the train again and Papa would meet us in the little Texas town of Colorado City. I was a little scared of our move but I didn't tell Mama.

Mama sometimes rode the streetcar to downtown Dallas to shop in the big stores. There won't be any big stores in the new town. Sometimes she would not let me peek into the sacks she carried home, and she tucked them away on a high shelf. She bought me a beautiful hat.

Grandpa and Grandma took me to have my picture made. I combed my long hair and wore the pretty new hat. We rode the streetcar. Mama said there would not be a photographer on the Plains, so I was glad I could have my picture made here in Dallas. I felt very special to have my picture made in a studio. It was exciting to see all the pretty people in the pictures on display on the walls of the studio. Maybe they would put my picture up in their display.

Grandpa helped me read, Aunt Matt taught me easy songs on her piano, and Grandma let me sew. I had been sewing a long time. I made a dress when I was six, yes I did. Mama helped me, of course. I peddled the machine very slow, like Mama said, and my scissors were not very sharp. We made a doll this summer. Mama sewed it from a pattern she ordered out of the newspaper. I helped stuff the doll with cotton and we made two dresses for her from scraps in Grandma's sewing basket. The red dress was my favorite. Aunt Matt painted the doll's face. She ended up looking kinda old, so I named her Grandma. I will take Grandma to our new home when we go.

It was fun at Grandpa's house but I missed Papa and my brothers. Papa's letter finally said that he would be ready for us to come soon. The mail hack took it to Amarillo where it came

21

by train to Dallas. We had been in Dallas since May and the summer was almost gone. I made two new friends. There was a little girl next door and Jane across the street. I was playing across the street with her when I heard Grandpa calling me. I pretended like I did not hear him call, "Mamie", until I saw that he had something in his hand. Then I ran home as fast as I could. It was my new book *Black Beauty*. He said I could take it to our new home. Maybe I could even read it on the train. I could read it to Kit. She would like that. I hoped she would say "streetcar" for Papa.

In early September, the day came to say goodbye and start our train trip to the Plains. We would travel to Colorado City and Papa and the boys would meet us in the wagon. I dressed myself in my gingham dress. Grandma packed me a lunch of hard-boiled eggs, a sandwich, and cookies. Grandpa gave me a nickel to buy candy on the train. Mama put the things Kit would need in the valise, so they would be handy. I was an experienced traveler by now and felt right at home boarding the train as I climbed up the stairs and found our seat.

When the train rolled into Colorado City, I was so excited that I jumped down the stairs and off the train and ran ahead of Mama. So I was the first to see Papa. Papa gave me a quick hug and hurried to help Mama and Kit down the train steps. What a happy reunion. I held hands with the boys and we jumped up and down in a circle. The boys were surprised to see how much the baby had grown. I was sure glad she gave them one of her big smiles.

I gave old Dan a big pat on his nose and slapped Rod's hip. I was happy to see my horse friends. Papa had the horses hitched to the wagon for our drive to Lubbock County. It was still daylight, so we started our 125 mile trip, driving the horses northwest. The wagon was full. Papa had bought lumber for our new house and it was stacked on the back. Mama sat up front with Papa and baby Kit. Dave, Bob, and I perched on the lumber, swinging our legs over the side.

The boys had so much to tell me about their trip in the spring. They had stopped by in a home where there were two boys very near their age. They hated to leave those new friends just like I hated to leave my girl friends in Dallas. When night came, Papa stopped at a house and talked to the man of the house and then he hollered to us, "Come on in and eat supper." The six of us went in for supper. Mama and Papa laid us

THIRSTY COWS

a pallet on the floor of their room and I fell asleep in a moment. That nice lady cooked us breakfast, while Papa and the boys tended the horses. We left early after telling the people we hoped they would stop in on us someday, in Lubbock County. We waved good-bye until they were out of sight.

Early in the morning I saw my first antelope. There was a small herd nearby and our wagon scared them. My, they were fast, as we watched them run away. Bob's constant chatter almost made my ears hurt, but it was fun to hear all about his new experiences. We soon came to a group of cute little animals. Bob said they were prairie dogs. They lived in holes in the ground and would stand on their back legs and bark. A ground owl lived in the holes with the prairie dogs. Dave told me how the prairie dogs ganged up on a rattlesnake. When the snake went into one of their holes, they began scraping dirt into it until they had the hole filled up. I loved seeing the sassy prairie dogs.

Papa would stop when we came to a spring or windmill with a dirt water tank. Horses drink lots of water. We kids were usually ready for a drink, too. There were lots of birds and snakes around the water. This traveling and camping was lots of fun for me but I could tell Mama and the baby were getting tired. We had been on our way for several days. When we camped out, Mama and Papa fried bacon and potatoes and cooked biscuits in the iron pot over a cow chip fire. We kids had to pick up dung chips for the fires. Our last night, we stayed in the O'Bannnons' home. They were a kind family, as was everyone whom we met along our way, and I was beginning to feel at home on the Plains.

SOD BUILDING IN TOWN

There weren't many houses in our new town. Papa said most of them had been moved from nearby Estacado. There were no trees for building on these plains and the lumber had to come in on the train to Colorado City. Some people built half dugout or sod houses. Mr. Hunt had a little one-room building for a store. He sold mostly groceries and a few household items. There was one building with an upstairs. Papa said this was used as a hotel. Our house was one large room and it was nice

I Could See Nothing

having all our family together again. Papa planned to build another room with the lumber we'd hauled home in the wagon. There was a wooden bed for Papa and Mama. We kids slept on the floor. Mama was happy to have an iron cook stove and there was glass in the windows. The community water well was a half-mile away. Dave and Bob hauled water in a little red wagon in 2 and 5 gallon buckets. We had a lovely neighbor, Mrs. Stevenson. She was elderly and we kids affectionately called her Grandma.

HALF DUGOUT

Our first school in Lubbock was a half dugout. Half dugouts were common buildings. A hole was dug in the ground about five feet deep. Timbers were placed around the hole on top of the ground to support the planks that covered the top. Sod and the excavated dirt covered the dug out. There was a little window in the back and a door with steps down to the floor. We had one teacher and there were about eight of us kids. She made twenty-five dollars a month. A potbelly stove stood in the center of the room and a long table with benches filled the rest of the space. We each had a pencil that Papa kept sharpened with his pocketknife and we had tablets to write on. My lunch box was a little syrup bucket. Bob would knock a clod of dirt off the wall and chunk it at his friend when the teacher was not looking. We all wore black, high top shoes. When the shoestrings broke and the local store ran out of shoestrings, we used thin rags or strings to keep the shoes on. We had long spells with no shoestrings to buy. On the morning after a supply wagon came into town, every kid in school would have new black shoestrings. We all looked neat again. The teacher always noticed that first thing as we popped down the stairs into the dug out.

The town people had a community meeting place in a one-room building. This building had a dirt floor but it was larger than a home. This would be where we'd decorate the community Christmas tree. I had worried about how we could have a Christmas tree because there were no evergreens on the Plains. But when Christmas came a real cedar tree stood in the meeting hall, decorated with strings of popcorn and a few gifts. Papa said two cowboys rode to the " breaks"– some distant hills with trees – especially to cut a tree for our Christmas. Christmas would not be Christmas without a tree! There were brush and comb sets, apples, and nuts under the tree, and pretty handkerchiefs decorated the branches. Five ladies in town knitted scarves for all the cowboys. This was a happy surprise for the men. There were a few wrapped gifts under the tree and we all hoped to find our names on a tag. There it was – "Mamie Crump" – a gift for me! I tore off the wrapping and there was the most beautiful doll in the world! Where had she come from? There were no dolls at our store. She had a bisque head with beautiful golden curls and bright blue eyes. I think this was the happiest Christmas of my life. The boys got marbles and books.

This first Christmas on the Plains was my greatest. I loved my doll and knew Mama must have bought her beautiful head in Dallas. Her body was just like my Grandma doll and they could wear the same dresses. Mama thinks of everything. Grandma Stevenson, next door, said my doll was the prettiest doll she had ever seen. I took extra good care of my doll and let my friends play only with my Grandma doll.

Bob was playing and teasing with our neighbor children, one day. He had my Grandma doll and they were tossing it around and pulling on it. I left the group and went inside with Mama. All of a sudden, Bob called out, "Grandma's neck is broken". Poor Mrs. Stevenson, Mama, and I rushed out to help. I was about to cry when I saw Grandma, or what was left of my poor rag doll. Her neck was hanging on by two threads. I was terribly angry because my doll was hurt. Mama calmly got out her sewing basket and soon had the head sewed on again. Thanks to her, everything was peaceful again.

COOKING ON THE PLAINS

Mary Lou Crump Koehler

A LIGHT SNOWFALL

I Could See Nothing

Chapter 4 Christmas Stories

Pioneers began arriving in Lubbock County on the Plains of Texas in the late 1800's and early 1900's. My family enjoyed making many new friends. People were isolated on the High Plains and pioneers turned to neighbors for companionship. The railroad in Amarillo was a long 125 miles away, three or four days of wagon travel. Neighbors stuck together and holiday celebrations were community projects. When Christmas approached, a few cowboys would ride many miles to cut an evergreen tree in the canyon below the Caprock. When they brought it back, a committee was on hand to trim the tree with strings of popcorn and paper chains. The Christmas tree was the center of interest in the new schoolhouse as the community gathered on Christmas Eve. There were sacks of oranges and apples for the children. An evening of singing and food ended with the arrival of Santa.

A Santa Claus suit was kept packed away in a trunk at the schoolhouse. The selection of a Santa could be a problem; it had to be a cowboy the kids would not recognize. Most of the cowboys were shy. This particular year, Sam, a bachelor and newcomer, was a perfect selection, the committee decided. It did take a couple of stiff drinks to convince Sam. The teacher, Miss Mary, helped him dress in the red and white outing flannel suit and poked a pillow into the jacket to give him a fat tummy. Cotton strips were glued to his chin and he made a pretty fair looking old gentlemen. He had to change his voice, so he popped a couple of coppers in his mouth and we all hoped he wouldn't choke on the darn coins.

WINTER ON THE PLAINS

The creaking wagons arrived on Christmas Eve, with the children huddled under quilts and singing carols as they jolted down the dusty two-rut road. There was no snow this year, so Santa elected to arrive on a white horse. Sam delayed his entrance until everyone was seated. Excitement built up as the children waited for Santa to arrive. They jumped up out of their seats squealing and giggling each time the front door opened. The laughs and shrieks were deafening when they finally heard a sleigh bell and a shout of "HO, HO, HO". "Merry Christmas" Sam hollered as he entered the room and we were off for a fun evening.

He swayed forward under the weight of his pack and made his way to the big trimmed tree. Once there, he started unloading that bulging sack and grownups handed out the gifts and fruit to the children. The fun evening finally drew to a close and wagons were being hitched up for the ride home. Two of the cowboys were in the corner laughing and slapping their legs and probably up to no good. Sam was having fun relaxing with his friends. The two prank-minded cowboys slipped up to Sam, struck a match and with a flash set Santa's beard on fire. The cotton blazed to his ears and smoke encircled his head. Sam froze with fear. Two men jumped up and tried to pull the cotton away, a finger pinch at a time, shaking their hands

I Could See Nothing

violently and dropping the bits of burning cotton to the floor. Seconds later, Miss Mary, the schoolteacher, grabbed her coat off the back of her chair ran to Sam and quickly wrapped the coat around Santa's face to smother the flames. Thanks to her quick action, his only injuries were singed hair and two blistered ears.

Sam was still suffering from shock and moaning about the near disaster next day at a neighbor's place. "Why those two stupid cowhands were picking the burning cotton off my chin like they had all day. If it hadn't been for Miss Mary, I would have burned alive."

"I don't know what you are fussing and stewing about, Sam," his friend drawled. "You came out ahead for one evening's work. You got yourself a thirty-five cent haircut plus a ten dollar hug."

Setting Santa on fire was an awful prank, not funny at all. I found myself involved in a prank years later that was almost as bad. I was a grown man and I should have known better. I was on the Christmas tree decorating committee and we were popping corn to string. A committee member told me about a community Christmas tree gathering in Oklahoma. She told how a duck was boxed and tagged for the local doctor. The air hole in the top of the box was large and every so often the duck would stick his head out of the box and give a "quack", "quack" as the gift waited under the tree. I suppose it was funny to everyone but perhaps the doctor.

This gave me a crazy idea; why not box a cat for the single, redheaded schoolteacher? The night of the community tree I found a black cat and put it in a box but the cat was quick to break out of the box with a lot of kicking and scratching. So I tied it in a gunnysack, tagged it for the teacher, and placed it under the Christmas tree. The cat scratched and rolled in the sack for awhile before it gave up and went to sleep. "You are in for it," declared a friend and until that remark I didn't think about the joke not being funny to all. This friend was right; I was in for it, all right!

BOB AND FRIENDS

Christmas gift time came and Santa was calling names and giving out gifts to the delight of the children. Then he picked up the cat sack and woke up the cat. The cat was scared and gave a loud meow. Santa said, "If there is an old maid in the house, this must be for her," and he read her name out, loud and clear. She jumped to her feet with fire in her eyes, took hold of the sack and slung it as hard as she could out of the open door. The cat sailed into the dark and hit one of the townsfolk right in the face. He'd been outside having a quiet smoke. He freed the scared cat and it ran off like a flash and Santa soon got the celebration going again.

She guessed it was I who sacked the cat for her and was heard to declare that she would like to "kick the seat of Bob's pants out his big mouth". Still, it was fun. It was five long years before we had another community Christmas tree.

Chapter 5 A Long Cold Day

I had often read of the respect and admiration given shepherds in foreign countries but in Texas, we were known as nothing more than a sheep herder. It was a good paying job for a boy of 15. I would bring home $15.00 for a month's work, but it did seem to be lacking in what we'd call "fringe benefits" today. The hours were long and lonesome and sometimes a week would go by before I'd see another human. Sleeping under the stars wasn't bad on a warm pallet in the bed of an old wagon that was missing the wheels, but my cooking was never going to win a prize. I cooked on a campfire of cow chips. I remember throwing a sour dough biscuit at a coyote one night and it sang through the air like a rock. My two greyhound dogs were good company. They chased rabbits for a meal and were fast enough to catch a coyote.

Bob's Greyhound

I rescued a baby antelope once; the coyotes had killed its mother. It became a favorite pet and would run and play with the dogs. I would tie the little one up near my bedroll at night. During the day he would follow the dogs and I as we watched the sheep. The boss and his wife visited me one day and she fell in love with the friendly antelope. She begged me for my pet and I let her take it back to the ranch house. I roped a snake one day with a fourth-inch cotton cord about ten feet long. He wiggled so hard that I let him go. The dogs barked at the snakes, prairie dogs, rabbits, and hawks as they swooped down. I had books to read, animals and birds to watch. Stars were bright at night and the golden sunset ended the day.

Winter finally arrived and was unusually cold for the Plains this year. The temperature was near zero. The boss sent a cowboy on horseback to help me bring the sheep back to the barns; it was too cold for them to graze. They had frozen ice balls on their wool and you could see their breath. The sheep were quick to settle down in the barn out of the cold and I took off for the house to warm up.

BOB'S PET ANTELOPE

The post office was nine miles away. The boss had not picked up his mail in several days and kept wishing for the mail as we sat around the fireplace. Eager to please, I saddled up a pony and was soon on my way to the post office, riding into the cold West Texas wind. I tied a big handkerchief over my nose to stop some of the cold. The ride home would seem shorter and warmer with the wind to my back, I figured.

I Could See Nothing

I stopped by my home to see Papa and Mama. Papa had been out working to fix a windmill and he gave me fits for being out in the extreme cold. It felt good to warm by the fire with the family. Mama fixed me a hot drink, and soon I was on my way to town again.

The news in town was about everyone's concern about the severe illness of a neighbor boy; friends were sitting up all night with him to give the family a rest. I sure hated to hear this. Jake was a good kid, just a few years younger than I. I dropped off the mail back at the ranch, warmed by the fire, then struck out walking to go see the sick friend. Their place was only a couple of miles away and the weather seemed too cold and windy to take the horse out again. After a week with the sheep, I would enjoy the visit.

Off For The Doctor

Jake was in bad shape. He was hot with fever and had a deep cough. Dr. Hunt, the local doctor, shook his head. He had done all he could do but he knew of a Doctor Wayland in Plainview that he hoped could help the boy. Plainview, Texas was a town about fifty miles to the north. I volunteered for the ride. The boss loaned me a horse when I got back, and I rode off across country for the first ten to fifteen miles before I hit the main road. This was the third day of extreme cold. The morning was quiet; it was too cold for the jackrabbits that usually ran from the horse. They must have been sleeping in their holes, staying warm.

The settlers along the way were friendly and trusting. I had no trouble trading my horse for fresh horses. On my return, I would leave each horse with the rightful owner. When I came to a barb wire fence, I would pull staples out of a couple of posts and stand on the wire to pull it down so I could ride over it. Then I'd put the wire back up. Mr. Landers' ranch was a little over half way. He had a bronc in his lot and I exchanged mine for it, to continue my ride. This horse was slow; I would have made better time if I had stayed on my pony. It took two horse changes and three and one half hours to reach the doctor's house. I explained the sad situation to Doc. It didn't take the doctor long to harness up his two horse rig. We tied the saddle pony on the back of the rig, tossed my saddle in the back, and drove the horses slow at first, giving them time to warm up. One of his horses became sick after a few miles; he slowed down and was tossing his head. Lucky for us, we saw a house nearby. We woke up the rancher and he loaned us a horse. There was an empty, warm stall where we could leave the sick animal. It was about eleven p.m. and the wind had eased up some by now but the temperature was still about zero. I noticed at the ranch a two-gallon bucket of water frozen solid. I was feeling tired from the strenuous day and kept tossing my arms and stamping my feet to help me stay warm.

The cold and darkness were hypnotizing. The doc's bag bounced out of the rig on the rough road and neither of us noticed. When we realized the bag was gone, we turned quickly to retrace our tracks and soon found the bag. Both of us regretted the lost time.

It was two a.m. when we sighted the light from Jake's family farmhouse. I felt so happy to get inside a warm place. Too late, too late, we learned the sad news. My friend had died two hours earlier. I gave his mother a hug. I had done my best and as I sadly turned to leave for home to check on the sheep and to sleep, I overheard two men talking about me. "That kid says he ain't cold but I know good and well he's frozen".

They were right.

Chapter 6 Wash Day

My ranch chores were many for a young cowpoke after I quit herding sheep and got a job as a ranch hand. Once every two weeks I was told to help the women folk with the clothes wash. Two big pots were set up in the back yard and filled with water. If we had rain we tried to catch and save enough rain water to fill one of them. A fire was built under the big black iron pot to warm the water. Homemade lye soap made of the grease from slaughtered hogs at killing time was shaved up and tossed into the water. A big galvanized tub held the rinse water. The rubbing board was used to rub dirty spots on the clothing clean. Give the spot a good lick with the soap and arm energy on the board and if you were lucky the spot would be gone. You had to remember to place the black iron pot where the smoke from the fire wouldn't blow in your face.

Wash Day

A broomstick handle was perfect to stir clothing in the hot water and lift the hot clothes into the rinse water. The boss's wife was a big, heavy woman and washing her long dresses with all their ruffles was like washing a wagon sheet. I would make three piles of clothes to wash, one pile colored, one pile white, and one pile britches and rags. More prosperous folks had a hand wringer to remove water but I hand twisted each piece. The rags we hung on the fence. The other clothing was hung on a wire that I'd strung from the windmill to the porch. When we were all through, the rinse water was poured on the flowerbed and the warm water was used to scrub the porch. It took almost all day to do the wash and at the end of the day the lady offered me a big cup of black coffee. There is nothing like the smell of clean clothes on wash day.

Chapter 7 Prairie Fire

West Texas ranchers feared prairie fires. The fire could burn huge sections of grassland. Fires usually started after the November freeze, which left the grass dead and dry. Flames were pushed by the strong, never-ending west winds. The only protection the ranchers had against the fires was to prepare fire guards. Early in the fall the guards were made by plowing two rows in the grass about fifteen feet apart. Grass in between the plowed rows was carefully burned off before the fire danger got too high. This created a bare area that would sometimes stop a fire. Lots of times, though, the fire was going fast enough to jump the barrier as sparks and burning debris blew across and landed in the dry grass on the far side.

Firefighters Ready For Battle

I remember this one fire really well. Black smoke billowed high, sounding its own alarm; prairie fire, prairie fire. That signal can be seen for many miles across the open flat plains of West Texas. The dreaded enemy skipped quickly across short grass left dry by the early winter freeze. The typical southwest wind pushed the flickering flames along rapidly, destroying valuable grass we needed to feed the livestock. The alarm automatically sends cowboys on horseback racing toward the dark cloud of smoke with only a saddle blanket or perhaps a rain slicker to try and beat out the hot flames.

At the ranch house the smoke was quickly spotted. Leather snapped as saddles were thrown on top of surprised horses, and the quick jerk of the girth strap warned animals of the urgency. Cowboys dipped all available gunnysacks into water troughs and tied them dripping to the backs of their saddles. These wet sacks would be used to slap out flames. At the foreman's order: "Ride to the fire," a newcomer spoke up: "The smoke is twenty miles away, Boss," he drawled.

"That is where we want to fight a prairie fire, cowboy." The foreman glared at him. "Twenty miles away – not on our ranch".

The women responded to the alarm as well. They grabbed their brooms, mounted and rode swiftly after the men, armed for the fight. Often a child bounced behind his mother and if it were not for the seriousness of the occasion, one would have to chuckle as the broom brigade galloped up to the battle. The household broom, strange as it seems, is an efficient firefighting tool. Sweeping it through short grass smothers flames and in thick, long grass, it is used to effectively pound out the fire.

The firefighters approached from behind the crackling blaze and scattered themselves along the complete line of fire if possible, beating, slapping, pounding, and sweeping without a thought for the heat and smoldering ground. Fires are fought from along the side and rear, as it is too dangerous to be in front of the fire. Large handkerchiefs tied around the nose and mouth help filter out smoke. Smoke burns your eyes, your shoes get hot and the heat blisters your face.

When flames seemed uncontrollable, in desperation, a yearling calf was roped and killed. The carcass was split open to lay flat and cowboys tied ropes to the left front and left hind legs. Two men on horseback raced along the fire line, dragging

I Could See Nothing

the bloody body flesh-side down through the flames. The wet carcass was a gruesome but effective tool against the fire. Cattle, antelope, and coyotes were defenseless. A skunk tried his natural defense on the fire but without success and raced off at top speed with a shabby, singed tail.

I remember how, in one fire fight, I had been in bed with a fever, but a prairie fire is no respecter of persons. My body spilled out of bed automatically as if it had forgotten its illness when the boss's call came. The old wind whipped flaming cow chips ten feet in the air; it seemed hard to believe that this uncontrolled fire had started from a family laundry – a small fire built under an iron wash pot to heat wash water.

I fought on, pushing fear from my mind, knowing good and well that the fifteen foot fire guards plowed and burned early in the fall would be no challenge for this fire. Where would it end? I cursed and prayed in the same breath. This was the worst I'd seen, the hottest, fastest and most hopeless – as long as the strong wind stayed in the southwest.

RELIEF FOR TIRED FIREFIGHTERS

"Hey, Bob, take a break," the foreman called out, and as I looked around, a wagon hauling water barrels lumbered up. I don't know which looked the best, the drinking water or the soaking wet gunnysacks. My throat had ached with thirst unnoticed until this minute and my sack was a blackened, burned mess. Blisters were popping up on my hands; my shirt was wet from sweat and my face black from the smoke.

The wagon soon rode on to other fighters leaving tracks on burnt grass and for a second I marveled at the efficiency of our unorganized, volunteer fire department. As I walked back to the flames I thought that somehow they seemed to be slowing or maybe I had drunk too much water. Sudden drops of water fell on my back and looking up in disbelief I saw a storm cloud above the black smoke. As the drops began to fall, I caught myself yelling, "Yip-ee, the old southwest wind is gone."

The flames were soon defeated but the work was not finished. Cowboys still had to ride the black, dead ground, watching for smoldering cow chips. Not this cowboy. The urgency had passed and my body felt sick again. I stopped in town to see Doc before returning to the ranch. The feeling of relief and gratitude after the flames had stopped was short lived. The town was filled with blackened faces, exhausted bodies, and depressed spirits. Twenty miles of grassland had been destroyed but the greatest loss was the stacks of feed that had been stored to feed the cows through the winter. Hardships were nothing new and somehow we would make do.

You just had to.

I waited my turn to see Doc and got a good check over. He pumped up the blood pressure cuff and stood there counting until a look of shock came over his face. "God, man, you ain't got none." He loaned me clean clothes that would have fit a man twice my size and home I rode hoping I could find my blood pressure.

Chapter 8 Fun and Games

Entertainment was an important part of community life for the early families on the West Texas Plains. Telephones were very few and far between. The women folk learned to use mirrors to contact family and friends. Sun reflecting off mirrors could be seen for miles because of the flat land. Sister Mamie would send reflections to signal a trip to town, a visit from a friend, or a party at the schoolhouse, in the jail, or dinner on the ground after preaching. School was moved to the jail after it was built. The jail was used as both the community center and the school, actually. It was seldom needed to hold a prisoner; folks were looking for homes not trouble.

TYPICAL PLAINS PICNIC

Sunday at the schoolhouse jail started with a union Sunday school followed by preaching if a traveling preacher was in town. A potluck lunch was served following church. The children played baseball, marbles, ran foot races, and tossed horseshoes. The older boys rode their horses to rope calves or tried to ride a bucking steer. Guys would rope a fence post if a calf wasn't available to practice roping. There was a cowboy called

Van, who had roped 365 calves at a spring branding round up without a single miss. This gave us boys a goal to work toward. Could we be as good as Van? Sundays usually ended with a sing-along. This left me on the outside on the steps; I can't carry a tune in a bucket. It was nice to spend the day with Papa and Mama and get a chance to swap yarns with friends.

STEER RIDING

Mamie and Mama enjoyed a sewing club. Quilting parties were held in the jail where there was room to spread a quilt and several women could work with their needles. The ladies enjoyed getting together to sew, talk, and share ideas. Mama was happy to share her sunbonnet pattern. Homemade items were prized and appreciated. I loved the shirts Mama made for me. She sewed them by hand in the years before we purchased a sewing machine that operated with foot power. Grandmother in Dallas had a sewing machine.

Mamie, Dave, and I attended the debating society meeting at the schoolhouse every month. I remember a question one night: "Is a horse and buggy more beneficial than the automobile?" The young man debating for the horse and buggy made his point. He could tie the horse lines to the wagon and the horses could wander slowly while he could hold his lady friend's hand and speak sweet words in her ear.

I Could See Nothing

Sunday Fun

Thanksgiving dinners were held at the school or in homes. Fresh garden vegetables were a blessing and thanks were given for the harvest. Turnips, cabbage, pumpkins, and potatoes could be stored for winter. Cellars or holes under the house would keep the vegetables for a few months. Four families would butcher a calf every month and each keep one fourth. The beef was hung from the windmill to dry and keep safe. We were thankful for good food. The community Christmas tree was special. There were picnics on the 4th of July and Dave and I would set off a few firecrackers.

Dances were fun, fun! A lighted coal-oil lantern was hung from the windmill to show the way to the host house since roads were mostly cow trails from one ranch to another. There were fiddles and a man named Jack who played the harmonica. If you could not dance you could always stomp your feet to the fiddling. Papa didn't dance but he would just about wear his leg out keeping time to the strains of "Turkey in the Straw," "The Arkansas Traveler," "Good-bye Old Paint," and "Cotton-Eyed Joe." The whole family was welcome and because the dance often lasted all night, the kids fell asleep in the wagons, listening to the music and counting falling stars.

The family moved to a new area twelve miles from Lubbock and helped start the town that is called Shallowater today. Mamie and I, as young adults, were asked to chaperone the younger generation on social outings. Dave left the plains for the Rio Grande Valley, where he started raising oranges and grapefruit.

FOURTH OF JULY WAGON RIDES

I remember one Fourth of July we took a wagon pulled by four mules into Lubbock for the celebration. The kids enjoyed the dancing and a few firecrackers were lit to end the evening. The sun was coming up as we drove the team and sleepy dancers home. We sometimes had picnics, candy pulls, and community wagon rides and the young people would laugh and sing as we rode along.

Summer was a time for a community barbecue. Everyone was invited and the day started early. The cowboys dug a pit and filled it with roots of the mesquite bush. Mesquites were about the only bushes growing on the plains and the grubs, as the roots were often called, made good firewood. Iron pipes were placed over the pit to hold chicken wire; this completed the grill. Rods with hooks on the ends were used to turn the heavy pieces of beef. A calf was butchered and quartered and the four quarters were roasted over the fire. Biscuits were baked in iron Dutch ovens. Ladies brought their favorite pies. The pies included egg custard, green tomato, dried apple, mincemeat, and buttermilk. Dried apple was my favorite. It was several years before fruit trees planted by the settlers produced fruit.

I Could See Nothing

Community Barbecue

I will share Mama's Green Tomato Pie recipe with you.

The stoves burned cow chips, and the ladies watched the pie closely until it was brown.

```
Green Tomato Pie
9 inch pie shell & top made with lard
Firm green tomatoes, to fill shell, peeled
1 cup sugar                              sliced
1 Tbsp Flour
3/4 tsp cinnamon
2 Tbsp vinegar
1 Tbsp water
2 Tbsp butter
Combine sugar, flour, cinnamon with tomatoes
& pour into pie shell. Sprinkle with vinegar
& water. Dot with butter. Top with top crust
Bake 400 for 10 minutes then reduce heat &
bake 25 to 30 minutes at 350 degrees
```

Green Tomato Pie

My favorite sport was hunting antelope. Antelope could be seen in droves of fifty or more in the late afternoon, grazing, running, and leaping in the pasture. If you brought one down, it was good food for the family. Jackrabbits were a small target but good eating when skinned and fried and good dog food.

Coyote hunting was both a necessity and a sport. There were lots of coyotes and they killed young calves and chickens. We learned to shoot at a young age but our parents stressed safety. There was a bounty on coyotes and this made me a little change.

It was a good life. We didn't have all the things that my grandparents had in Dallas, but we had a lot of fun. Papa was right. That "nothing nothing" land turned out to be pretty special for all of us.

MAMIE AND BOB

Epilogue

I hope you have enjoyed this account of my father's early years on the Plains. Papa, W.D. Crump, was the third judge in Lubbock County. He ranched, farmed, and in later years had a branch of the County Library in his home. He died at age ninety-five in 1940. I was in second grade.

MARY LOU AND NOVELLA WITH PAPA

Mama, Mary King Crump, died a few years before I was born. I have often wondered how her parents felt sending their daughter and grandchildren to the Plains. Her father, Dr. David King, was one of the pioneer physicians in Dallas County.

MARY LOU CRUMP KOEHLER

Dave Crump left the Plains and bought a small citrus farm in Mission, Texas near his Aunt Matt King Turley.

Mamie and Kit were teachers in the Lubbock area. Kit, Katie Bell Crump, was honored for thirty seven years of service by the Lubbock council of Parent Teacher Association (PTA).

Bob, my Dad, farmed and raised registered Hereford cattle. He and my mother visited me every year in Oregon. We would sit around the kitchen table and talk about his experiences growing up. I jotted down details as he enjoyed sharing his stories.

My husband, David, daughters Lou Anna and Celia, sister Novella Hart, and Mary Rosenblum encouraged and assisted me with this story and the pictures.

Mary Lou Crump Koehler

I Could See Nothing

Life on The Plains

CPSIA information can be obtained
at www.ICGtesting.com
Printed in the USA
LVHW091132151020
668792LV00027B/198/J

9 780998 970431